Althea's Window Box
and the
Land of Slumber

Written by J. L. Britsas

Illustrated by Mason Parker

Illustrated by Mason Parker

Edited by Rachel Lee Lidskog
Layout by Anita Jones, Another Jones Graphics

ISBN: 978-0-9843295-0-2
Library of Congress Control Number: 2009913016

Publisher's Cataloging-In-Publication Data
(Prepared by The Donohue Group, Inc.)

Britsas, J. L.
   Althea's window box and the land of slumber / written by J. L. Britsas ;
illustrated by Mason Parker.

     p. : ill. ; cm.

   Summary: A city girl dreams that she journeys into the wilderness. Along the way
she encounters opportunities and challenges that require her to adapt to the new
surroundings. In this adventure of discovery she builds strength, courage,
appreciation, character and heart.
   Interest age level: 002-007.
   ISBN: 978-0-9843295-0-2

1. City children--Juvenile fiction. 2. Nature--Juvenile fiction. 3. Dreams--
Juvenile fiction. 4. City children--Fiction. 5. Nature--Fiction. 6. Dreams--
Fiction. I. Parker, Mason. II. Title.

PZ7.B758 Al 2010
[E]   2009913016

ITSAS1202
PRODUCTIONS

Printed in the USA

Dedicated to Kris

Whose dream became an inspiration.

Althea's school bus stops near the Princess Apartments.

This is where her grandma lives.

She runs through the front door and up three flights of stairs.

Althea loves her grandma.

When the chores were all finished, and her homework was done,

Althea would gather her friends and open a book.

She would read story after story, and look through picture books too,

of the beautiful world, the stars, sun and the moon...

about far away places, mountains, rivers and trees...

"Yes, I want us all to go there," she'd say,

"but today...we can dream."

It was cozy, very cozy on their big cushioned perch...

with pillows and a blanket, being warmed by the sun.

Althea would grow sleepy and nod off to sleep.

The flowers in the window box would be the last thing she'd see.

Althea opened her eyes onto a beautiful spring day,

and what a surprise...could it be?

"At last...we have arrived!"

With a heart full of joy, she began to run.

Fragrant-flowers perfumed the valley air,
and a blur of colors passed quickly by.

She came to rest at the side of a shallow stream.

The water was clear and cool .

Althea could see fish swimming and some frogs.

"If I were a fish, what would I see?"

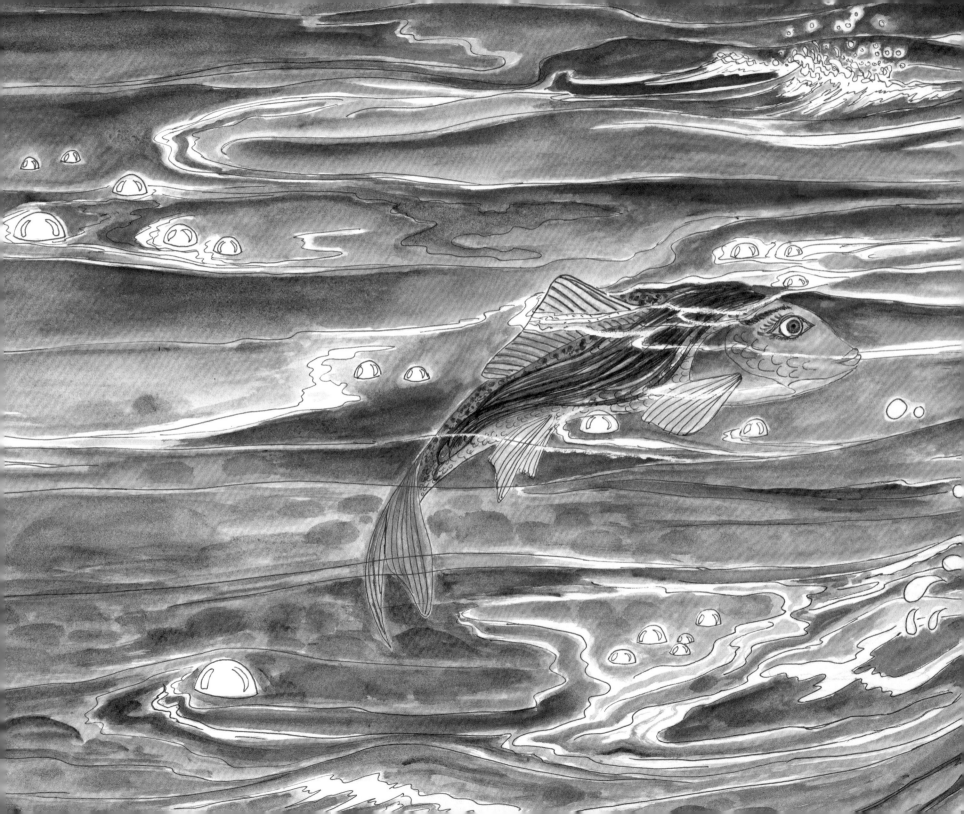

The water in the stream moved slowly at first,
but as it spilled into the rapids, it became rough and fast.

Althea was brave.

She drifted into a calm cove where a mountain lion crouched
on the shore to drink.

It turned and followed a path through the trees.

"I wonder where he is going?"

"I wonder what we will see."

The path became very steep. Rocks had replaced the trees,

And the sun was bright in the reaching blue sky.

Althea was strong and followed the steep path up and up and up...

"This must be the top of the world!"

Althea was lifted high in the air and soared

A majestic hawk cradled by the warm winds.

With out-stretched wings they glided,

in large swirling circles,

to the desert floor.

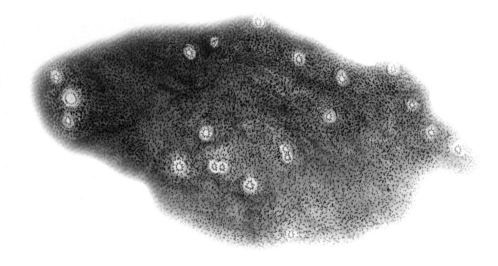

A few friends sat waiting for her there.

It had been a long journey. Althea was tired.
She lay on the warm ground and gazed into the night's sky.

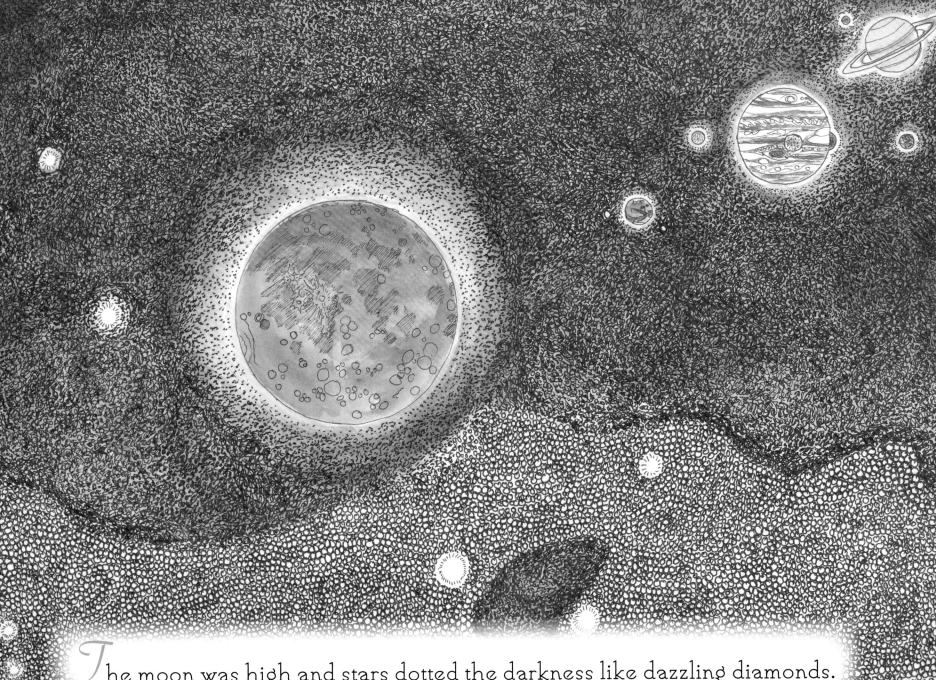

The moon was high and stars dotted the darkness like dazzling diamonds.
"Where shall we go now?" she wondered.

"Althea...supper's ready."

A familiar voice called from Afar...

Soon Grandma would hear stories of
Althea's wondrous windowbox adventure.

Jason Britsas – Author

"As a native of San Diego, California I found inspiration in the diverse geographical surroundings. In a single day I could spend time swimming in the ocean, hiking in the mountains and exploring the desert wilderness.
My story book celebrates the vast beauty that is available to us every day."

Find Jason at: www.itsas1909.com or itphonix@live.com

Mason Parker – Artist

"Having been used to 'live' sessions where I have buildings, trees, and people going about their business before me, this book has given me the challenge of putting greater emphasis on human and animal figures in scenes, while still paying due attention to the overall picture. It is a new exercise in drawing/painting from photos and creating imaginary scenes with them. My scenes are drawn with waterproof pen and followed with watercolors. This allows me to be thorough with details and generous with colors. I use Arches paper or the equivalent."

Find Mason at: www.masonscreations.com or sonofthespiralshop@yahoo.com